Pokey Is Sick

Story by Debbie Croft

Illustrations by Debbie Mourtzios

Tess got out of bed
and went into the kitchen.

"Pokey!" she said
to her little puppy.
"Are you sick?
You look sick to me!"

"Here is some water, Pokey,"
said Tess.

Pokey looked up at Tess.

Pokey stayed in her basket.

Danny came into the kitchen.

"Pokey is sick, Danny," said Tess.
"She will not get out
of her basket."

Danny looked at Pokey.

"I'm going outside to play
in the yard," said Danny.
"I will get the ball.
Pokey likes running after it."

"Pokey cannot go outside today,"
said Tess.
"She is too sick!"

Danny got the ball.

Pokey looked at Danny,
and she got out of her basket.

"Look, Tess!" said Danny.

"Pokey is not sick.

Her nose is cold and wet.

She **can** come outside with me.

You can come outside, too."

"Look at Pokey," shouted Tess.

"She is running!

She is not sick at all."